THIS BOOK
BELONGS TO

_____

Raymond's Uncut Diamond

A. M. MARCUS

Raymond felt very sad. He was thinking about what the other children had said about him at school.

"BORING!"

He wondered if perhaps they were right...maybe he was useless and boring.

5

Raymond needed advice.
So, he decided to go visit
his wise Grandpa, who
lived just down the lane.

"Come in!"

nock!

Knock!

Raymond reached Grandpa's house and knocked on the door. Knock! Knock! "Come in!" said Grandpa.

Raymond entered and immediately started talking. "It seems that I am not good for anything, and I don't know what to do!"

Grandpa replied, "Hello, Raymond! I'd like to give you my full attention, but right now I'm quite busy."

Grandpa continued, "If you will help me with something first though, then I'd be very happy to help you with your problem."

12

Raymond answered eagerly, "Sure, Grandpa! How can I help you?"

"Go and sell this stone at the market," said Grandpa, "but be sure not to sell it for less than one gold coin."

Happily, Raymond made his
way to the market.

As he walked, he thought about how he could help Grandpa sell the stone, and hoped that Grandpa could then help him with his problem.

Raymond tried his best to sell the stone for one gold coin, but had no success.

After several hours, one man offered to buy the stone for just two silver coins.

But, Raymond remembered what Grandpa had said, so he refused the man's offer and kept trying to get one gold coin.

In the evening, a nice older gentleman approached Raymond and explained to him, "My boy, a gold coin is too high a price for such a simple stone."

Grandpa listened as Raymond told all about his disappointing day.

Then Grandpa said, "Well, tomorrow maybe we can find out the real value of this stone!"

Raymond nodded as Grandpa told him, "Perhaps the jeweler is the right person to judge the stone's worth, so take it to him. However, make sure you don't sell the stone to him. No matter what he says, bring the stone back to me."

The next day, Raymond took the stone to the jewelry store.

JEWELRY STORE

He asked the jeweler about its value and watched as the jeweler examined the stone carefully.

"Hmmm, I can offer you 100 gold coins for it," stated the jeweler, as he handed the stone back to Raymond.

"Wow!" exclaimed Raymond, surprised.

Running back to Grandpa's house,
Raymond was excited as he thought
about the jeweler's wonderful news.

As soon as Raymond arrived, he eagerly told Grandpa what had happened in the jewelry store.

Grandpa smiled and explained,

"If you take a good look, you can see this is not just an ordinary stone, Raymond. It is an uncut diamond, thus only a professional jeweler would know its true worth."

"Did you know that you are like this uncut diamond, Raymond?" Grandpa told him. "You should see what a properly cut diamond looks like! I have one in the back...wait just a minute!"

Grandpa searched for a little while, and came back with a dazzling diamond. When Raymond saw it, he was shocked!

43

Then Grandpa put the uncut diamond in Raymond's left hand and the other one in his right hand, and told him to look at them carefully.

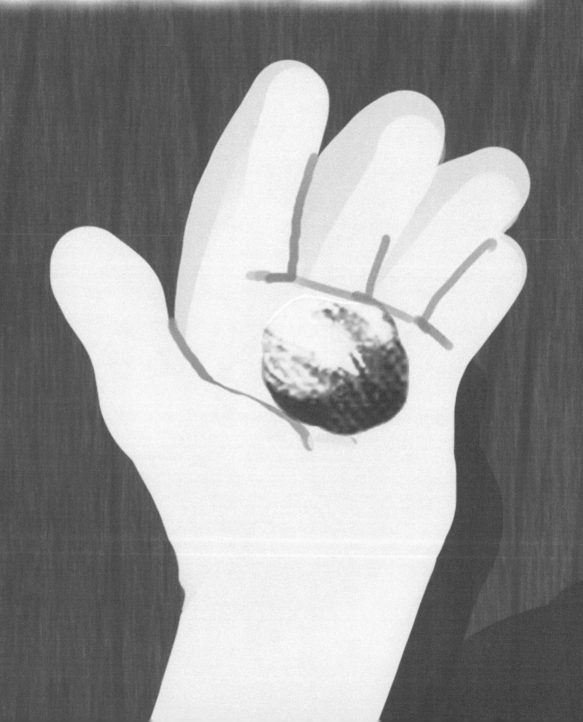

Grandpa explained, "You see, the uncut diamond represents you right now, and the well-cut diamond is the potential of what you can become!"

"Just as all the people in the market did not know the real value of the diamond, perhaps you and your schoolmates, and even some grownups cannot see your true value."

Grandpa continued, "Only the people who know diamonds really well, like a jeweler, understand their true value."

"However, your family knows you very well, and WE know that *you* ARE a diamond, but the most important thing of all is that **you have to know it inside yourself!**"

49

50

Raymond looked at the well-cut diamond and thought about himself and his potential.

51

He was excited to think
of shining just like the
beautiful diamond.

Raymond was so glad that Grandpa had helped him with his problem and had given him this new understanding.

When he returned to school and saw
his schoolmates, he felt confident,
because he knew deep in his heart
his true value.

THE END

I wish that someone had asked me the questions I am about to ask you when I was younger. I know you are very smart and can think for yourself. How would you answer these questions?

• Has a person ever said something and as you thought about their words you felt useless or unimportant? Does that person know you well?

• Can someone who doesn't know you very well really know your worth?

• Do you think your family, especially your parents, know you best and understand your true value and potential?

• What are one or two things that you want to do or become that are difficult for you?

• Will it require a lot of hard work and determination to accomplish these goals? Will it be worth it?

I would love to know what you think of my book!
Please send me an email: author@AMMarcus.com
or share your thoughts with the rest of the world on Amazon.

Scan and post a review

A word from me to the grown-ups

As parents, helping our children develop positive self-esteem and confidence is one of the best gifts we can give them. Children who are inspired to think of their own potential and self-worth know that they are loved and have the tools to reach for their dreams and goals.

I hope this book has reinforced for your children the importance of trying hard to become better in everything they do. When others discourage them or they feel that they are not so good at something, it is a parent's privilege to use that opportunity to lift up their children's heart. By letting them know that not being good at something is only a temporary state and by encouraging them to work hard to fulfill their potential, we are equipping our children with a "can-do" attitude that will help them succeed in life.

I hope I have inspired both you and your children.
If you liked this book, would you consider posting a review?
Your help in spreading the word is greatly appreciated. Reviews from readers like you make a huge difference in helping new readers find children's books with powerful lessons similar to this book.

I would love to hear from you! Please subscribe to my email newsletter following the link on the last page. In the newsletter you will find exciting updates, promotions, and more.

Follow this direct link to post a review

go.ammarcus.com/raymond-review

My favorite fruits: Strawberries & Raspberries

My favorite school subjects: Math & Computers

My favorite hobby: Dancing & Teaching Salsa

My favorite color: Green

My favorite animal: Tiger

My favorite sport: Soccer

My favorite pet: Dogs

Don't forget your
FREE GIFT
on the last page

I graduated from the Technion Israel Institute Of Technology with B.Sc. Cum Laude in Computer Engineering. Throughout my studies, I have been teaching and helping children with math, and through my work, I have helped them to discover their inner strength and motivation to continue studying and nurturing success in life.

I love the challenge of early education, and especially enjoy working with children with learning difficulties. I have found great satisfaction in helping them conquer their fears and overcome the challenges associated with their education.

I have read dozens of self-improvement books, and have been influenced heavily by them. Through self-reflection, I have found that my great dream was to share that wisdom and my numerous life lessons with people, but especially with kids.
I left my computer engineering career in order to pursue my dream of becoming an author of children's books. Today, I continue to write these books, with the goal of teaching kids basic skills through storytelling. I believe that a good story is an excellent way to communicate ideas to children.

Each and every story is based upon some deep issue, value, or virtue that can potentially make a huge impact on the lives of both your children and you. I have a vast collection of quotes, and usually I base my stories off quotes that I personally find inspiring. The lesson of this book, for example, can be summed up in the following inspirational quote by author Joice Meyer. Turn the page to check the quote.

www.AMMarcus.com

"Potential is a priceless treasure, like gold. All of us have gold hidden within, but we have to dig to get it out."

-Joyce Meyer, Author

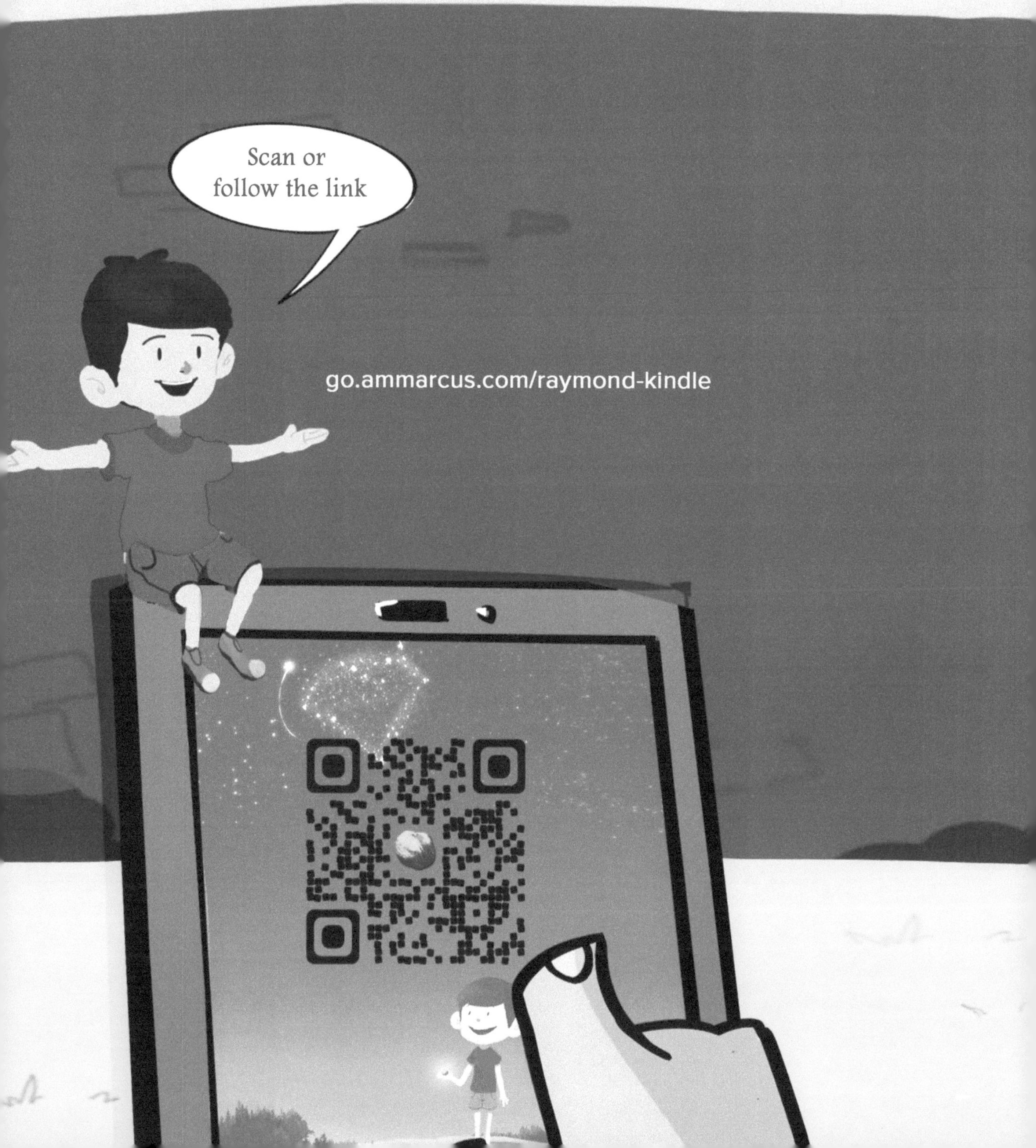
Scan or follow the link
go.ammarcus.com/raymond-kindle

Coming soon!

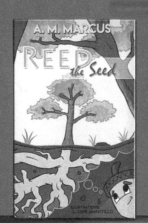

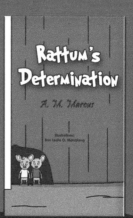

**Don't forget
your FREE GIFT**

Scan to get your
FREE GIFT

ammarcus/free-gift

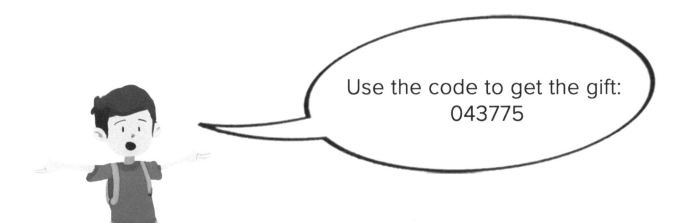

Use the code to get the gift:
043775

Printed in the USA
CPSIA information can be obtained
at www.ICGtesting.com
LVHW070409240823
756124LV00003B/11

* 9 7 8 1 5 1 8 7 8 8 5 1 2 *